A LIFT-THE-FLAP BOOK

CORDUROY'S BIRTHDAY

SCHOLASTIC INC.
New York Toronto London Auckland Sydney

Today is Corduroy's birthday! He is very excited.
After breakfast he checks his mailbox. There are three
birthday cards and a note. The note says that Corduroy
should come to Checkerboard Bunny's house at three o'clock.
Who tied those balloons to Corduroy's mailbox?

Corduroy wonders what he can do until three o'clock.
He decides to clean up. He recycles his newspapers
and donates clothes that no longer fit him to the children's
shelter. Corduroy has grown a lot this year!
He also chooses some cans of food for the food bank.

Corduroy's friends are busy, too. They are planning a surprise party for Corduroy. They are making a cake, some cards, and birthday decorations. *Sshhhhh*—don't tell Corduroy!

It's three o'clock!
Corduroy knocks on Che
Where could Checkerboa
SURPRISE! HAPPY BIR

Now it's time to play some games.
Who will break the piñata?
Isn't that clown funny?

Corduroy's friends have planned a treasure hunt.
Who will find the most treasure?

Finally it's time for the birthday cake.
Corduroy makes a wish before he blows out the candles.
Happy Birthday, Corduroy!

DON FREEMAN was born in San Diego, California, and moved to New York City to study art, making his living as a jazz trumpeter. Following the loss of his trumpet on a subway train, Mr. Freeman turned his talents to art full-time. In the 1940s, he began writing and illustrating children's books. His many popular titles include *Corduroy*, *A Pocket for Corduroy*, *Beady Bear*, *Dandelion*, *Mop Top*, and *Norman the Doorman*.

LISA McCUE was born in Tappan, New York, and has illustrated more than seventy-five books, including *Corduroy's Halloween*, *Corduroy's Christmas*, *Corduroy's Toys*, *Corduroy's Day* and *Corduroy on the Go*. She lives in Bethlehem, Pennsylvania, with her husband and their two sons.

ISBN 0-590-39876-8

Text copyright © 1997 by Penguin Books USA Inc. Illustrations copyright © 1997 by Lisa McCue. All rights reserved. Published by Scholastic Inc., 555 Broadway, New York, NY 10012, by arrangement with Viking Penguin, a division of Penguin Books USA Inc. SCHOLASTIC and associated logos are trademarks and/or registered trademarks of Scholastic Inc.

12 11 10 9 8 7 6 5 4 3 2 1   7 8 9/9 0 1 2/0

Printed in Singapore   46

First Scholastic printing, September 1997

Set in Stempel Garamond